# Dear Parents:

Congratulations! Your child is taking the first steps on an exciting journey. The destination? Independent reading!

**STEP INTO READING®** will help your child get there. The program offers five steps to reading success. Each step includes fun stories and colorful art or photographs. In addition to original fiction and books with favorite characters, there are Step into Reading Non-Fiction Readers, Phonics Readers and Boxed Sets, Sticker Readers, and Comic Readers—a complete literacy program with something to interest every child.

## Learning to Read, Step by Step!

### Ready to Read   Preschool–Kindergarten
• big type and easy words • rhyme and rhythm • picture clues
For children who know the alphabet and are eager to begin reading.

### Reading with Help   Preschool–Grade 1
• basic vocabulary • short sentences • simple stories
For children who recognize familiar words and sound out new words with help.

### Reading on Your Own   Grades 1–3
• engaging characters • easy-to-follow plots • popular topics
For children who are ready to read on their own.

### Reading Paragraphs   Grades 2–3
• challenging vocabulary • short paragraphs • exciting stories
For newly independent readers who read simple sentences with confidence.

### Ready for Chapters   Grades 2–4
• chapters • longer paragraphs • full-color art
For children who want to take the plunge into chapter books but still like colorful pictures.

**STEP INTO READING®** is designed to give every child a successful reading experience. The grade levels are only guides; children will progress through the steps at their own speed, developing confidence in their reading. The F&P Text Level on the back cover serves as another tool to help you choose the right book for your child.

Remember, a lifetime love of reading starts with a single step!

*To Connie, an apple of a friend!*
*—C.R.*

*This one goes to my families:*
*The one in Mexico, the one in France,*
*and the one at Bright.*
*And to Jan, who taught me well in* Pumpkin
*so I could breeze through* Apple!
*—E.M.*

Text copyright © 2016 by Candice Ransom
Cover art and interior illustrations copyright © 2016 by Erika Meza

Visit us on the Web!
StepIntoReading.com
randomhousekids.com

Educators and librarians, for a variety of teaching tools, visit us at RHTeachersLibrarians.com

*Library of Congress Cataloging-in-Publication Data*
Ransom, Candice F., author.
Apple picking day! / by Candice Ransom ; illustrated by Erika Meza.
    pages  cm. — (Step into reading. Step 1)
Summary: "A family spends a day at an apple orchard." —Provided by publisher.
ISBN 978-0-553-53858-8 (trade pbk.) — ISBN 978-0-553-53859-5 (lib. bdg.) —
ISBN 978-0-553-53860-1 (ebook)
[1. Stories in rhyme. 2. Apples—Fiction.] I. Meza, Erika, illustrator. II. Title.
PZ8.3.R1467Ap 2016
[E]—dc23
2015011571

Printed in the United States of America
10 9 8 7 6 5 4 3 2 1

This book has been officially leveled by using the F&P Text Level Gradient™ Leveling System.

# Apple Picking Day!

by Candice Ransom

illustrated by Erika Meza

Random House 🏠 New York

In the morning
we leave town.

Drive past woods
all gold and brown.

Over hill tops,
big and small.

I see apples.

Hello, fall!

Tractor takes us
to the trees.

I spot ladders
in the leaves.

Run down this row.

Follow me!

Lots of apples
on that tree.

I pick high.

You pick low.

In our basket
apples go.

Hungry blue jay
flaps and hops.

Jabs a bad one.
Down it drops.

Share an apple.

Hey, my turn.

Crunch, crunch, munch.
Yuck! A worm!

See that apple
way up there?

On my tiptoes
I grab air!

I try again.

Down come two.

One for me
and one for you.

Boy in that tree
makes a face.

Quick, pick faster!
Start a race!

# Tractor pulls us
# to the shed.

We sort apples
green and red.

Apple cider.

Apple pie.

# Apple donuts
# hot and fried.

Fun day over.
We love fall!
Yummy apples,
best of all.